Dear Parent:

Congratulations! Your child is taking the first steps on an exciting journey. The destination? Independent reading!

STEP INTO READING® will help your child get there. The program offers five steps to reading success. Each step includes fun stories and colorful art. There are also Step into Reading Sticker Books, Step into Reading Math Readers, Step into Reading Phonics Readers, Step into Reading Write-In Readers, and Step into Reading Phonics Boxed Sets—a complete literacy program with something to interest every child.

Learning to Read, Step by Step!

Ready to Read Preschool–Kindergarten
• big type and easy words • rhyme and rhythm • picture clues
For children who know the alphabet and are eager to begin reading.

Reading with Help Preschool–Grade 1
• basic vocabulary • short sentences • simple stories
For children who recognize familiar words and sound out new words with help.

Reading on Your Own Grades 1–3
• engaging characters • easy-to-follow plots • popular topics
For children who are ready to read on their own.

Reading Paragraphs Grades 2–3
• challenging vocabulary • short paragraphs • exciting stories
For newly independent readers who read simple sentences with confidence.

Ready for Chapters Grades 2–4
• chapters • longer paragraphs • full-color art
For children who want to take the plunge into chapter books but still like colorful pictures.

STEP INTO READING® is designed to give every child a successful reading experience. The grade levels are only guides. Children can progress through the steps at their own speed, developing confidence in their reading, no matter what their grade.

Remember, a lifetime love of reading starts with a single step!

For Suzy, who loves him so!
—G.H.

Copyright © 2011 by Geoffrey Hayes

All rights reserved.
Published in the United States by Random House Children's Books, a division of Random House, Inc., New York.

Step into Reading, Random House, and the Random House colophon are registered trademarks of Random House, Inc. |\ / \|

Visit us on the Web!
StepIntoReading.com
www.randomhouse.com/kids

Educators and librarians, for a variety of teaching tools, visit us at
www.randomhouse.com/teachers

Library of Congress Cataloging-in-Publication Data
Hayes, Geoffrey.
A poor excuse for a dragon / by Geoffrey Hayes.
   p. cm. — (Step into reading. A step 4 book)
Summary: When Fred the dragon leaves home, he learns that he is not very good at roaring or breathing fire, and swallowing people only makes him ill, but with help from a witch, a giant, and a wise boy he finds his true calling.
ISBN 978-0-375-87180-1 (hardcover) — ISBN 978-0-375-86867-2 (trade pbk.)
ISBN 978-0-375-96867-9 (lib. bdg.) — ISBN 978-0-375-89938-6 (ebook)
[1. Dragons—Fiction.] I. Title.
PZ7.H31455Poo 2012
[E]—dc22   2010025000

Printed in the United States of America
10 9 8 7 6 5 4 3 2 1

A Poor Excuse
for a Dragon

by Geoffrey Hayes

Random House 🏠 New York

When Fred was old enough to leave home, his father and mother gave him a list.

How to Be a Good Dragon
Run amok
Eat people
Roar
Breathe fire
Act scary

"I'll miss your beautiful red eyes," said Mom.

"Make us proud of you," said Pop.

"I'll try," said Fred.

At noon, he came to a wide green field.
It looked like the perfect place to run amok.
Fred began running in circles. He
waved his arms. He roared and knocked
over haystacks. But it only made him dizzy.

He had to lie down for a few minutes!

Soon, he smelled something yummy.
"Where is that smell coming from?"
said Fred.

He went to find out.

The smell was coming from a castle.

Fred waded across the moat so he could peep over the wall.

Mrs. Green, the cook, was busy in the kitchen. She had left a plate of pancakes on the windowsill.

Fred wondered if they tasted as yummy as they smelled.

He looked at his list: *Eat people.*

"Nuts!" said Fred.

He climbed over the castle wall.

When Mrs. Green came into the garden
to pick strawberries, Fred jumped in front
of her and roared.

Mrs. Green got a look on her face.
"Who let *you* in?"

"I am the Dragon with Two Red Eyes,
and I'm going to eat you!" cried Fred.

"You may have two red eyes, but your
roar sounds like a meow!" said Mrs. Green.

"I'll show *you,*" said Fred.

He swallowed Mrs. Green in one gulp.

He didn't even take time to chew her.

"Let me out at once, or I'll tell the princess," said Mrs. Green.

"Won't!" said Fred.

He heard someone coming.

It was Princess Viniver.

"Yoo-hoo! Mrs. Green? When will brunch be ready?" she called.

Fred hid in the bushes.

He checked his list: *Breathe fire.*
This will be fun, thought Fred.

He ran from behind the bushes and spit fire.

"I am the Dragon with Two Red Eyes, and I'm going to eat you!"

Princess Viniver giggled. "You may have two red eyes, but your fire looks like a birthday candle."

"I'll show *you*!" cried Fred.

He swallowed Princess Viniver in one gulp. He didn't even take time to chew her.

"So, you're in here, too," Mrs. Green said when she saw the princess.

"Let us out or we'll scream at the top of our lungs," cried Princess Viniver and Mrs. Green.

"Won't!" said Fred.

Fred heard someone knocking at the castle door. He poked his head around the wall.

A small bird had come to sing to
Princess Viniver.

I'll act really, really *scary this time,*
thought Fred.

Fred ran out. He waved his arms.
He spit fire. He gave his biggest roar!

"I am the Dragon with Two Red Eyes,
and I'm going to eat you!"

"You may have two red eyes," said the bird, "but you don't scare me."

"I'll show *you*!" said Fred.

He swallowed the bird in one gulp.

It was getting crowded inside the dragon's tummy.

"He'll be inviting the *squirrels* in next," said Mrs. Green.

"This stinks!" said Princess Viniver. "Now I'll never get my pancakes!"

She looked so sad that the bird sang a song to cheer her up.

"Stop singing," said Fred. "I'm trying to be scary."

"Won't!" said the bird.

Suddenly, Fred didn't feel so good.

He wandered into the forest, sat under a tree, and groaned.

The Hooty Witch, who had been up all night inventing spells, was trying to take a nap.

She ran out of her cottage waving her arms.

"Go groan someplace else," said the Hooty Witch. "I need my rest."

"I can't," said Fred. "My tummy hurts."

"I have something that will help," said the Hooty Witch.

She disappeared inside her cottage and came out with a huge bottle of castor oil.

"Here," she said. "Drink this."

Fred swallowed the entire thing, bottle and all.

"Castor oil! Yuck!" cried Princess
Viniver, Mrs. Green, and the bird. They
tossed the bottle of castor oil back out.

"What on earth was that?" asked the
Hooty Witch.

Fred told the Hooty Witch the whole
story.

"No wonder your tummy hurts!" she
said. "Castor oil won't help. We need to go
see the Giant."

"Oh, no!" cried Princess Viniver, Mrs. Green, and the bird. "Not the Giant!"

"It's for your own good," said the Hooty Witch.

"I suppose swallowing us was for our own good, too," said Mrs. Green.

The Hooty Witch led Fred over rocks, through trees, and up the hill to the Giant's cave.

The Giant was in the middle of playing checkers with himself and didn't like being bothered.

"This better be worth my time," he said.

"I am the Dragon with Two Red Eyes,"
said Fred. "We need your help."

He told the Giant the whole story.

"Didn't your mother ever tell you to
chew your food?" said the Giant. "Well,
what do you want *me* to do?"

"Could you reach down my throat with your long arm and pull everybody out?" asked Fred.

"I can try," said the Giant. "But if you bite my arm off, you'll soon be the Dragon with Two *Black* Eyes!"

The Giant stuck his arm down Fred's throat. There was a lot of yelling from inside Fred's tummy.

The Giant pulled his arm back out.

"This won't work!" cried Fred. "You're choking me!"

"We had better go see John Little," said the Giant. "He's the smartest boy I know."

John Little was herding sheep.

"Why didn't I just eat a sheep?" said
Fred. "I'm sure *that* would have agreed
with me."

"Sheep are yummy!" said the Giant.
"I like mine with a little mint sauce."

"Hello, Giant!" called John Little.
"Who are your friends?"

They told John Little the whole story.

John Little thought for a minute. Then
he went into the barn and came out with a
big stick and a very long rope.

"Now, my dear," John Little said to the
dragon, "lie down on your tummy and
don't move."

As soon as Fred lay down, John Little
propped his mouth open with the big stick.

He tied one end of the very long rope
to a tree. He tied the other end around
his waist.

He told the Hooty Witch and the Giant,
"When I say *pull,* I want you to pull on this
rope as hard as you can."

"Sure thing!" they answered.

John Little crawled into Fred's mouth and down his throat. He found Princess Viniver, Mrs. Green, and the bird huddled in a corner.

"There's no more room in here," said Mrs. Green. "So you had better crawl right back out!"

"I plan to," said John Little. "And I'm
going to take you all with me."

"What a hero!" cried Princess Viniver.

"Suppose the Giant eats us?" said the
bird.

"The Giant is a friend of mine,"
answered John Little. "He won't eat you.
And even if he does, you'll be no worse
off than you are now."

Everyone agreed.

John Little told them to get down on their knees and to make themselves as small as possible. They each grabbed on to the rope, and John Little yelled, "Pull!"

The Giant and the Hooty Witch pulled
as hard as they could and . . .
BINGO!

In no time, everybody was sitting on the grass outside. The bird was so happy, he composed a song on the spot!

"Oh, that feels better!" said Fred. "I'm sorry I swallowed you. I've made a real mess of things! I guess I'm a poor excuse for a dragon."

Mrs. Green pulled Princess Viniver aside. They began whispering. Fred tried to listen.

He heard Princess Viniver say, "Well, it's worth a shot."

They went over to Fred, and Princess Viniver said, "Mrs. Green and I were wondering if you would like to come live in the moat. I've been pestering Mrs. Green for a House Dragon. And you would be perfect!"

"But my roar is like a meow. My fire is like a birthday candle. And I'm not scary," said Fred.

"Nonsense! How many dragons have such scary red eyes?" said Mrs. Green.

Fred hadn't thought of that.

"Will I get pancakes?" he asked.

"As many as you like," said Princess Viniver.

"Then I'll do it!" said Fred.

So John Little went back to herding his sheep,

the Giant went back to his checkers, and

the Hooty Witch went back to her nap.

Fred gave up running amok to
live in the moat.

Mrs. Green cooked more pancakes.
And everybody was happy.

Fred sent his mother and father a letter:

CASTLE CURIOUS

DEAR MOM AND POP,
   YOU WILL BE VERY PROUD OF ME.
I HAVE A JOB AS A HOUSE DRAGON.
I PROTECT THE CASTLE WITH MY
TWO RED EYES. I DON'T EAT PEOPLE
ANYMORE. I PREFER PANCAKES.